Table of Contents

How to Use This Book

This Premium Education Series workbook is designed to suit your teaching needs. Since every child learns at his or her own pace, this workbook can be used individually or as part of small group instruction. The activity pages can be used together with other educational materials and are easily applied to a variety of teaching approaches.

Contents

A detailed table of contents lists all the skills that are covered in the workbook.

Units

The workbook is divided into units of related skills. Numbered tabs allow you to quickly locate each unit. The skills within each unit are designed to be progressively more challenging.

Activity Pages

Each activity page is titled with the skill being practiced or reinforced. The activities and units in this workbook can be used in sequential order, or they can be used to accommodate and supplement any educational curriculum. In addition, the activity pages include simple instructions to encourage independent study, and they are printed in black and white so they can be easily reproduced. Plus, you can record the child's name and the date the activity was completed on each page to keep track of learning progress.

Practice Test

A comprehensive practice test helps prepare the child for standardized testing in a stress-free environment. Presented in the fill-in-the-circle format, this test includes skills covered on standardized tests.

Answer Key

The pages in the back of the workbook provide answers for each activity page as well as the practice test. These answer pages allow you to quickly check the child's work and provide immediate feedback on how he or she is progressing.

Beginning s

The beginning sound in **seal** is spelled with the letter **s**.

<u>s</u>eal

Say the name of each picture. Circle the pictures in each row that have the same beginning sound as **seal**.

1.

2.

3.

4.

5.

Beginning t

Name_____ Date_____

The beginning sound in **turkey** is spelled with the letter **t**.

_turkey

Say the name of each picture. Circle the pictures in each row that have the same beginning sound as **turkey**.

1.

2.

3.

4.

5.

Name_____ Date_____

The beginning sound in **bicycle** is spelled with the letter **b**.

<u>b</u>icycle

Name the pictures. Write **b** below each picture that has the same beginning sound as **bicycle**.

1.

2.

Write **b** to complete each word. Say the word.

 3. ___ell

 4. ___ird

 5. ___oy

 6. ___ed

Beginning h

Name_____ Date_____

The beginning sound in **hamburger** is spelled with the letter **h**.

hamburger

Say the name of each picture. Color the pictures in each row that have the same beginning sound as **hamburger**.

1.

2.

3.

4.

5.

Premium Education Language Arts: Grade I   6   © Learning Horizons

Name_____ Date_____

The beginning sound in **mouse** is spelled
with the letter **m**.

mouse

Say the name of each picture. Write **m** below each picture that has
the same beginning sound as **mouse**.

 1._____

 2._____

 3._____

4._____

 5._____

- - - - - -   - - - - - -   - - - - - -   - - - - - -   - - - - - -

 6._____

7._____

 8._____

 9._____

 10._____

- - - - - -   - - - - - -   - - - - - -   - - - - - -   - - - - - -

 11._____

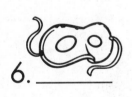 12._____

 13._____

 14._____

 15._____

- - - - - -   - - - - - -   - - - - - -   - - - - - -   - - - - - -

Name_____ Date_____

The beginning sound in **king** is spelled
with the letter **k**.

king

Say the name of each picture. Write **k** below each picture that has
the same beginning sound as **king**.

 1._____

 2._____

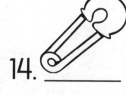 3._____

 4._____

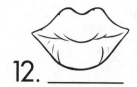 5._____

 6._____

 7._____

 8._____

 9._____

 10._____

 11._____

 12._____

 13._____

 14._____

15._____

Beginning Sound Practice (1)

Name_____ Date _____

Say the name of each picture.
Circle the letter that stands for the beginning sound.

1. 	2. 	3. 	4. 
h b	b t	m s	k b
5. 	6. 	7. 	8. 
t b	k t	h m	s t
9. 	10. 	11.	12. 
m t	b k	s h	m k
13. 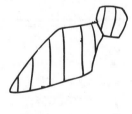	14. 	15. 	16. 
h s	t b	m b	t s

Name_____ Date_____

The beginning sound in **jack-o-lantern** is spelled
with the letter **j**.

jack-o-lantern

Say the name of each picture. Circle the pictures in each row that
have the same beginning sound as **jack-o-lantern**.

1.

2.

3.

4.

Name_____ Date_____

The beginning sound in **fox** is spelled with the letter **f**.

fox

Say the name of each picture. Color the pictures in each row that have the same beginning sound as **fox**.

1.

2.

3.

4.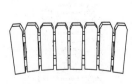

Beginning g

Name_____ Date_____

The beginning sound in **gift** is spelled
with the letter **g**.

gift

- -

Say the name of each picture. Write **g** below each picture that has
the same beginning sound as **gift**.

1. _____   2. _____   3. _____   4. _____

- - - - - -   - - - - - -   - - - - - -   - - - - - -

5. _____   6. _____   7. _____   8. _____

- - - - - -   - - - - - -   - - - - - -   - - - - - -

Look at each picture. Write a word that starts with **g** to finish each rhyme.

a _____ **in a coat**

a loose _____

Name_____ Date _____

The beginning sound in **lamb** is spelled with the letter **l**.

lamb

Say the name of each picture. Circle the pictures in each row that have the same beginning sound as **lamb**.

1.

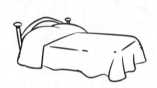

2.

3.

4.

Name_____ Date _____

The beginning sound in **duck** is spelled
with the letter **d**.

duck

Say the name of each picture. Write **d** below each picture that has
the same beginning sound as **duck**.

1. ____

- - - - - - - -

_____

2. ____

- - - - - - - -

_____

3. ____

- - - - - - - -

_____

4. ____

- - - - - - - -

_____

5. ____

- - - - - - - -

_____

6. ____

- - - - - - - -

_____

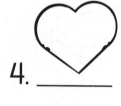

7. ____

- - - - - - - -

_____

8. ____

- - - - - - - -

_____

9. ____

- - - - - - - -

_____

10. ____

- - - - - - - -

_____

11. ____

- - - - - - - -

_____

12. ____

- - - - - - - -

_____

13. ____

- - - - - - - -

_____

14. ____

- - - - - - - -

_____

15. ____

- - - - - - - -

_____

Beginning n

Name_____ Date_____

The beginning sound in **nest** is spelled with the letter **n**.

<u>n</u>est

Say the name of each picture. Write **n** below each picture that has the same beginning sound as **nest**.

 1._____

 2._____

 3._____

 4._____

 5._____

 6._____

 7._____

 8._____

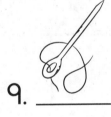 9._____

 10._____

 11._____

 12._____

 13._____

 14._____

15._____

Beginning Sound Practice (II)

Name_____ Date_____

Say the name of each picture. Fill in the circle next to the letter that stands for the sound you hear at the beginning.

1.
○ m
○ j
○ r

2.
○ n
○ p
○ d

3.
○ r
○ f
○ l

4.
○ n
○ k
○ p

5.
○ f
○ s
○ w

6.
○ y
○ l
○ m

7.
○ g
○ j
○ w

8.
○ s
○ k
○ d

9.
○ t
○ m
○ j

10.
○ j
○ h
○ n

11.
○ g
○ d
○ f

12.
○ f
○ y
○ l

Name_____ Date _____

The beginning sound in **witch** is spelled with the letter **w**.

witch

Say the name of each picture. Write **w** below each picture that has the same beginning sound as **witch**.

 1. _____
- - - - -

 2. _____
- - - - -

 3. _____
- - - - -

 4. _____
- - - - -

 5. _____
- - - - -

 6. _____
- - - - -

 7. _____
- - - - -

 8. _____
- - - - -

Look at each picture. Write a word that starts with **w** to finish each rhyme.

 a pig in a _____
- - - - - - - -

a dragon in a _____
- - - - - - - - - -

Beginning c

Name_____ Date _____

The beginning sound in **cat** is spelled
with the letter **c**.

<u>c</u>at

- -

Say the name of each picture. Color the pictures in each row that
have the same beginning sound as **cat**.

1.

2.

3.

4.

5.

Beginning r

Name_____ Date_____

The beginning sound in **rabbit** is spelled with the letter **r**.

rabbit

Say the name of each picture. Circle the pictures in each row that have the same beginning sound as **rabbit**.

1.

2.

3.

4.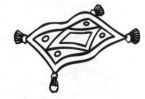

Name_____ Date_____

The beginning sound in **pig** is spelled with the letter **p**.

pig

Say the name of each picture. Circle the pictures in each row that have the same beginning sound as **pig**.

1.

2.

3.

4.

5.

Beginning q

Name_____ Date_____

The beginning sound in **queen** is spelled
with the letter **q**.

queen

Say the name of each picture. Write **q** below each picture that has
the same beginning sound as **queen**.

1. _____

_____

2. _____

_____

3. _____

_____

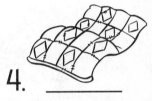

4. _____

_____

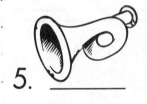

5. _____

_____

6. _____

_____

7. _____

_____

8. _____

_____

9. _____

_____

10. _____

_____

11. _____

_____

12. _____

_____

Name_____ Date _____

The beginning sound in **violin** is spelled
with the letter **v**.

<u>v</u>iolin

Say the name of each picture. Color the pictures in each row that
have the same beginning sound as **violin**.

 1.

2.

3.

Write **v** to finish each word.

4.  ____ an   5.  ____ est

6.  ____ alley   7. ____ ase

Name_____ Date _____

Say the name of each picture. Fill in the circle next to the word that names the picture.

1.
   ○ rig
   ○ pig

2.
   ○ pat
   ○ cat

3.
   ○ vest
   ○ pest

4.
   ○ raccoon
   ○ caccoon

5.
   ○ pie
   ○ vie

6.
   ○ vuilt
   ○ quilt

7.
   ○ can
   ○ van

8.
   ○ wug
   ○ rug

9.
   ○ vencil
   ○ pencil

10.
    ○ volcano
    ○ wolcano

11.
    ○ quell
    ○ well

12.
    ○ robot
    ○ wobot

Beginning x, y, and z

Name_____   Date_____

The beginning sound in **x-ray** is spelled with the letter **x**.

The beginning sound in **yak** is spelled with the letter **y**.

The beginning sound in **zoo** is spelled with the letter **z**.

Say the name of each picture. Write **x** below the picture that has the same beginning sound as **x-ray**. Write **y** below the picture that has the same beginning sound as **yak**. Write **z** below the picture that has the same beginning sound as **zoo**.

1. _____

2. _____

3. _____

4. _____

5. _____

6. _____

7. _____

8. _____

9. _____

10. _____

11. _____

12. _____

Ending d and g

Name_____ Date _____

The sound at the end of **sad** is spelled with the letter **d**.

The sound at the end of **pig** is spelled with the letter **g**.

Say the name of the first picture in each row.
Circle the other pictures in the row that end with the same sound.

1.

2.

3.

4.

5.

Unit 1

Name_____ Date_____

The sound at the end of **fan** is spelled with the letter **n**.

The sound at the end of **net** is spelled with the letter **t**.

Say the name of each picture. Fill in the circle next to the letter that stands for the sound you hear at the end.

1. ○ n ○ t	2. ○ n ○ t	3. ○ n ○ t	4. ○ n ○ t
5. ○ n ○ t	6. ○ n ○ t	7. ○ n ○ t	8. ○ n ○ t
9. ○ n ○ t	10. ○ n ○ t	11. ○ n ○ t	12. ○ n ○ t
13. ○ n ○ t	14. ○ n ○ t	15. ○ n ○ t	16. ○ n ○ t

Ending x and p

Name_____ Date_____

The sound at the end of **six** 6 is spelled with the letter **x**.

The sound at the end of **soap** is spelled with the letter **p**.

Say the name of the first picture in each row.
Color the other pictures in the row that end with the same sound.

Name_____ Date _____

The sound at the end of **drum** is spelled with the letter **m**.

The sound at the end of **sub** is spelled with the letter **b**.

Say the name of the first picture in each row.
Circle the other pictures in the row that end with the same sound.

Ending s, k, and r

Name_____ Date _____

The sound at the end of **yes** 👍 is spelled with the letter **s**.

The sound at the end of **hook** 🪝 is spelled with the letter **k**.

The sound at the end of **car** 🚗 is spelled with the letter **r**.

Say the name of each picture. Fill in the circle next to the letter that stands for the sound you hear at the end.

1.	2.	3.	4.
○ s ○ k ○ r	○ s ○ k ○ r	○ s ○ k ○ r	○ s ○ k ○ r
5.	6.	7.	8.
○ s ○ k ○ r	○ s ○ k ○ r	○ s ○ k ○ r	○ s ○ k ○ r
9.	10.	11.	12.
○ s ○ k ○ r	○ s ○ k ○ r	○ s ○ k ○ r	○ s ○ k ○ r
13.	14.	15.	16.
○ s ○ k ○ r	○ s ○ k ○ r	○ s ○ k ○ r	○ s ○ k ○ r

Name_____ Date _____

Say the name of each picture.
Circle the letter that stands for the sound you hear at the end.

1.	2.	3.	4.
n d	d t	g d	t g

5.	6.	7.	8.
d b	k s	g b	f m

9.	10.	11.	12.
b t	s m	k x	r s

13.	14.	15.	16.
g m	d g	p n	d t

17.	18.	19.	20.
k r	p b	x k	t p

Short Vowel a (1)

Name_____ Date _____

The word **hat** has a short **a** sound.

h<u>a</u>t

Say the name of each picture.
Color the pictures in each row that have the short **a** sound.

1.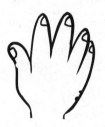

2.

3.

4.

Name_____ Date_____

Say the name of each picture.
Circle the word that names the picture.

1. 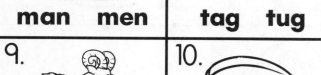	2.	3.	4.
cat cut	cap cup	hit hat	can cin

5.	6.	7.	8.
man men	tag tug	mop map	pan pin

9.	10.	11.	12.
rim ram	clom clam	hand hund	met mat

13.	14.	15.	16.
van ven	rat rit	fan fun	jum jam

17. 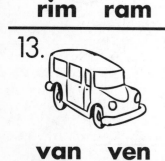	18.	19.	20.
bat bit	bag bug	him ham	limp lamp

Name_____ Date _____

Read the words in the box.
Write a word from the box to complete each sentence.

Unit 2

| bat | cat | fat | flat | rat | sat |

1. The white _____ is sleeping on my lap.

2. A small _____ is eating cheese.

3. Our car has a _____ tire.

4. I _____ on the chair.

5. Tim is up to _____ with two outs.

6. Look at the _____ pig!

Words with -an

Name_____ Date_____

Read the words in the box.
Write a word from the box to complete each sentence.

Dan fan man pan ran van

_____
- - - - - - - - - -

1. Jan _____ to catch the bus.

_____
- - - - - - - - - -

2. We will ride in the green _____ .

_____
- - - - - - - - - -

3. My brother _____ likes to eat jam.

_____
- - - - - - - - - -

4. If it is hot, turn on the _____ .

_____
- - - - - - - - - -

5. Mom put the ham in a _____ .

_____
- - - - - - - - - -

6. When he grows up he will be a _____ .

Name_____ Date_____

The word **pin** has the short **i** sound.

p<u>i</u>n

Say the name of each picture. Circle the pictures in each row that have the short **i** sound.

1.

2.

3.

4.

5.

Short Vowel i (II)

Name_____ Date _____

The word **dig** has the short **i** sound.

dig

Say the name of each picture.
Circle the word that names each picture.

1. pin pen	2. hill holl	3. kung king	4. mix max
5. sax six	6. kick kack	7. pig peg	8. mutt mitt
9. laps lips	10. chin chun	11. crab crib	12. watch witch
13. twig twug	14. fan fin	15. wig wag	16. bib bub

Name_____ Date_____

Read the words in the box.
Write a word from the box to complete each sentence.

chin	fin	pin	spin	twin	win

1. I like to watch the top _____.

2. The fish has a big _____.

3. She has a _____ sister.

4. The team will _____ the game.

5. The man has hair on his _____.

6. _____ the tail on the donkey.

Name_____ Date _____

Read the words in the box.
Write a word from the box to complete each sentence.

| big | dig | jig | pig | twig | wig |

_____

1. Did you see the _____ roll in the mud?

2. I saw the little elf dance a _____ .

3. Does the bald witch wear a _____ ?

4. Let's _____ a hole to plant the tree.

5. The pretty bird sat on a _____ .

6. A _____ dog jumped the gate.

Name_____ Date _____

The word **cup** has the short **u** sound.

c<u>u</u>p

Unit 2

Say the name of each picture. Color the pictures in each row that have the short **u** sound.

1.

2.

3.

4.

5.

Short Vowel u (II)

Name_____ Date _____

The word **up** has the short **u** sound.

up

Say the name of each picture.
Circle the word that names the picture.

1. **bug bag**	2. **deck duck**	3. **cub cab**	4. **nut net**
5. **jig jug**	6. **rag rug**	7. **sun sin**	8. **cup cap**
9. **tub tib**	10. **gem gum**	11. **cat cut**	12. **drum drom**
13. **sib sub**	14. **hog hug**	15. **thumb thimb**	16. **cuff caff**

Name_____ Date _____

Read the words in the box.
Write a word from the box to complete each sentence.

| cub | rub | scrub | stub | sub | tub |

1. The baby _____ sleeps in a cave.

2. The _____ moves underwater.

3. Jan put the pup into the _____ to bathe it.

4. Mom will _____ the pan.

5. The genie will come if you _____ the lamp.

6. It hurts to _____ your toe.

Words with -ug

Name_____ Date _____

Read the words in the box.
Write a word from the box to complete each sentence.

| bug | hug | tug | mug | plug | rug |

1. The pup likes to _____ on the rope.

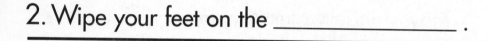

2. Wipe your feet on the _____ .

3. Dad will _____ in the lamp.

4. Mom drinks coffee out of a _____ .

5. Yuk! There is a _____ on my cup!

6. I like to give my mom a _____ .

Short Vowel o (1)

Name_____ Date _____

The word **pot** has the short **o** sound.

p<u>o</u>t

Say the name of each picture. Color the pictures in each row that have the short **o** sound.

1.

2.

3.

4.

5.

Name_____ Date_____

The word **sock** has the short **o** sound.

s<u>o</u>ck

Say the name of each picture.
Circle the word that names the picture.

1. ox ax	2. bix box	3. map mop	4. lock lick
5. clack clock	6. pet pot	7. top tap	8. knit knot
9. pop pip	10. hip hop	11. cat cot	12. jag jog
13. frig frog	14. leg log	15. doll dill	16. rock ruck

Words with -og

Name_____ Date_____

Read the words in the box.
Write a word from the box to complete each sentence.

| dog | fog | frog | hog | jog | log |

1. My _____ barks at the mailman.

2. I like to _____ around the block.

3. Can you jump over that _____?

4. Tom found a _____ in his yard.

5. The fat _____ won first prize at the County Fair.

6. The _____ was very thick in the morning.

Name_____ Date_____

Read the words in the box.
Write a word from the box to complete each sentence.

| drop | hop | mop | pop | shop | stop |

_____

1. Can you _____ on one foot?

_____

2. The car will _____ for walkers.

_____

3. Cindy loves to _____ .

_____

4. The red balloon did not _____ .

_____

5. The janitor will _____ the floor.

_____

6. Did the player _____ the ball?

Short Vowel e (1)

Name_____ Date_____

The word **bell** has the short **e** sound.

b**e**ll

Say the name of each picture. Circle the pictures in each row that have the short **e** sound.

1.

2.

3.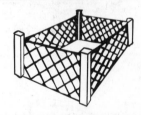

4.

5.

Name_____ Date _____

The word **egg** has the short **e** sound.

<u>e</u>gg

Say the name of each picture.
Circle the word that names the picture.

1. bid bed	2. leg lag	3. ball bell	4. tent tant
5. balt belt	6. well will	7. twelve twulve	8. nat net
9. pun pen	10. nast nest	11. desk duck	12. pat pet
13. driss dress	14. man men	15. jat jet	16. web wib

Words with -et

Name____________________ Date__________

Read the words in the box.
Write a word from the box to complete each sentence.

bet	jet	met	pet	wet	yet

1. Sam has a ____________ turtle.

2. She ____________ me at the store.

3. The ____________ flew high in the sky.

4. I did not clean my room ____________ .

5. It is so much fun getting ____________ .

6. I'll ____________ I can run faster than you.

Name_____ Date _____

Read the words in the box.
Write a word from the box to complete each sentence.

| **Ben** | **hen** | **pen** | **ten** | **then** | **when** |

_____

1. The farmer fed his _____ .

_____

2. I have _____ cents.

_____

3. _____ are we going to Grandma's house?

_____

4. A pig got out of the _____ .

_____

5. I will eat lunch, and _____ I will watch T.V.

_____

6. _____ likes to play soccer.

Short Vowel Practice

Name_____ Date_____

Say the name of each picture.
Fill in the circle next to the correct word.

1.

- ○ tan
- ○ ten
- ○ tin

2.

- ○ rig
- ○ rag
- ○ rug

3.

- ○ sax
- ○ sox
- ○ six

4.

- ○ fan
- ○ fen
- ○ fin

5.
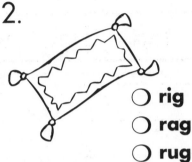
- ○ pan
- ○ pen
- ○ pin

6.
- ○ bax
- ○ bex
- ○ box

7.
- ○ leg
- ○ lig
- ○ log

8.

- ○ hat
- ○ hit
- ○ hot

9.

- ○ pag
- ○ peg
- ○ pig

10.
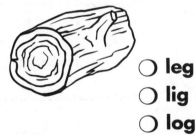
- ○ tub
- ○ tab
- ○ teb

11.

- ○ wab
- ○ web
- ○ wib

12.

- ○ bad
- ○ bed
- ○ bib

Word Family Practice

Name_____ Date _____

Read each sentence. Circle the word that best completes the sentence. Write the word on the line.

1. Fran lost her _____ rabbit.	**Pat** **pet** **pig**
2. The man can _____ a hole.	**big** **jig** **dig**
3. The little _____ sat on the rock.	**mug** **hop** **frog**
4. Dad will buy a new red _____ .	**rat** **set** **van**
5. The _____ went down to the bottom of the ocean.	**sub** **tan** **cub**
6. _____ will we go to the zoo?	**Men** **When** **That**
7. Tom likes to _____ across the rocks.	**hop** **mop** **win**

Long Vowels with Silent e

Name_____ Date_____

When silent **e** is added to some words, the first vowel makes a **long** sound.

can   can**e**

Say the name of each picture. Add **e** at the end of each word. Then circle the picture of the new word.

1. **cap**    cap___

2. **tap**   tap___

3. **pin**   pin___

4. **tub**    tub___

Read each word.
Write two words from the box to complete each sentence.

| plan |
| plane |
| not |
| note |

5. The _____ can _____ fly today.

6. I _____ to write a _____ .

Long Vowel a (I)

Name_____ Date _____

Say the name of each picture. Circle the word that names the picture. Then write the word.

1.  gate
   gas

   _____

2.  plane
   pan

   _____

3. 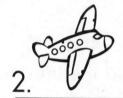 rat
   rake

   _____

4.  lake
   lamp

   _____

5.  tag
   tape

   _____

6. snap
   snake

   _____

7. cast
   cake

   _____

8.  skate
   scat

   _____

9. cane
   can

   _____

10. cave
    cane

    _____

11. wag
    wave

    _____

12. cap
    cape

    _____

Name_____ Date_____

The **long a** in the word **train** is spelled **ai**.

tr**ai**n

Write **ai** to finish each word. Read the words.

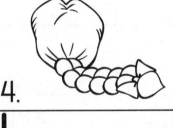
1. sn___l

2. p___l

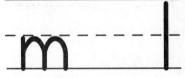
3. t___l

4. br___d

5. s___l

6. m___l

7. r___n

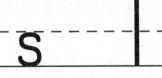
8. n___l

9. p___nt

Name_____ Date _____

The **long a** in the word **tray** is spelled **ay**.

tr**ay**

Read the words. Write a word from the box to complete each sentence.

day	gray	hay	May	pay	stay

1. The black horse eats _____ .

2. He will _____ for the candy.

3. Our little _____ cat is lost.

4. What _____ are we going to Grandma's house?

5. _____ I please have a glass of milk?

6. We must _____ here and wait for Mom.

Name _____ Date _____

Say the name of each picture.
Write a word for the second picture that rhymes.

Unit 3

1.

cake _____

2.

gray _____

3.

trail _____

4.

cave _____

5.

jay _____

6.

chain _____

Long Vowel i (l)

Name_____ Date _____

The word **slide** has the **long i** sound.

slide

Say the name of each picture. Color the pictures in each row that have the **long i** sound.

1.

2.

3.

4.

5.

Name_____ Date _____

The word **nine** has the **long i** sound.

9

n_ine

Say the name of each picture.
Circle the word that names the picture.

1.

fine   five

2.

mice   mine

3.

slip   slide

4.

dive   dig

5.

hide   hive

6.

pin   pie

7.

book   bike

8.

dice   does

9.

kite   kit

10.

dim   dime

11.

bride   bread

12.

pick   price

13.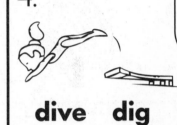

Vinny   vine

14.

turn   tire

15.

tie   top

16.

pipe   pile

Name_____ Date _____

Say the name of each picture. Write a word for the second picture that rhymes. Use the words in the box.

| bride | dime | hive | kite | mice | tie |

1.

_____

_ _ _ _ _ _ _ _ _ _

white _____

2.

_____

_ _ _ _ _ _ _ _ _ _

pie _____

3.

_____

_ _ _ _ _ _ _ _ _ _

lime _____

4.

_____

_ _ _ _ _ _ _ _ _ _

dive _____

5.

_____

_ _ _ _ _ _ _ _ _ _

price _____

6.

_____

_ _ _ _ _ _ _ _ _ _

slide _____

Name_____ Date _____

Read the words.
Write a word from the box to complete each sentence.

bite	**hike**	**line**	**mine**	**time**	**wipe**

1. We went for a _____ in the mountains.

2. Write your name on the _____ .

3. What _____ do you have to leave?

4. Please _____ the table after eating lunch.

5. Someone took a _____ out of my sandwich.

6. That video is _____, not yours.

Long Vowel u (1)

Name_____ Date _____

The word **fruit** has the **long u** sound.

fr**ui**t

Say the name of each picture. Circle the pictures in each row that have the **long u** sound.

1.

2.

3.

4.

Premium Education Language Arts: Grade 1   **62**   © Learning Horizons

Name_____ Date _____

Say the name of each picture.
Fill in the circle next to the word that names the picture.

Unit 3

1.
- ○ Tusk
- ○ Tuesday
- ○ Tune

2.
- ○ tub
- ○ tube
- ○ tap

3.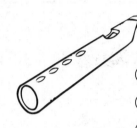
- ○ flat
- ○ flute
- ○ fly

4.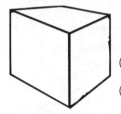
- ○ cub
- ○ cube
- ○ clock

5.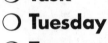
- ○ clap
- ○ club
- ○ clue

6.
- ○ juice
- ○ jump
- ○ junk

7.
- ○ bring
- ○ bruise
- ○ brush

8.
- ○ frog
- ○ frame
- ○ fruit

9.
- ○ mule
- ○ must
- ○ milk

10.
- ○ top
- ○ tug
- ○ tune

11.
- ○ gum
- ○ glue
- ○ grab

12.
- ○ sun
- ○ suit
- ○ sip

Name_____ Date_____

Read the words. Write a word from the box to name each picture.

bruise	clue	cruise	cube	flute	fruit
glue	juice	prune	rude	suit	tube

1.
_____

2.
_____

3.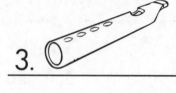
_____

4.
_____

5.
_____

6.
_____

7.
_____

8.
_____

9.
_____

10.
_____

11.
_____

12.
_____

Name_____ Date _____

Read each sentence. Circle the word that best completes the sentence.
Write the word on the line.

_____ - - - - - - - - - 1. I can play a _____ on my flute.	**tune** **rule** **use**
_____ - - - - - - - - - 2. My birthday is in the month of _____ .	**Tuesday** **June** **Ruth**
_____ - - - - - - - - - 3. She will wear her new _____ dress.	**cube** **blue** **dude**
_____ - - - - - - - - - 4. Do you want to go for a _____ ride?	**prune** **hue** **mule**
_____ - - - - - - - - - 5. The library book is _____ today.	**due** **tube** **cute**
_____ - - - - - - - - - 6. Is that story _____ or made up?	**blue** **glue** **true**
_____ - - - - - - - - - 7. Mom put an ice _____ in my glass.	**clue** **cube** **cruise**

Unit 3

Long Vowel o (1)

Name_____ Date_____

The word **coat** has the **long o** sound.

c**oa**t

Say the name of each picture. Color the pictures in each row that have the **long o** sound.

1.

2.

3.

4.

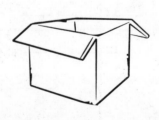

Name_____ Date_____

The word **hoe** has the **long o** sound.

h**oe**

Say the name of each picture. Circle the word that names the picture.

Unit 3

1.

   doe   down

2.

   cane   cone

3.

   note   nut

4.

   coal   could

5.

   glob   globe

6.

   soap   sob

7.

   cot   coat

8.

   home   hut

9.

   test   toast

10.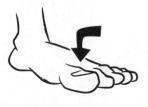

    toe   town

11.

    rob   robe

12.

    boat   bop

Name_____ Date_____

Read the words. Write a word from the box to name each picture.

boat	cone	doze	hole	nose	pole
road	rope	rose	snow	stove	toad

1.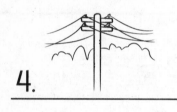
_____
- - - - - - - - -
_____

2.
_____
- - - - - - - - -
_____

3.
_____
- - - - - - - - -
_____

4.
_____
- - - - - - - - -
_____

5.
_____
- - - - - - - - -
_____

6.
_____
- - - - - - - - -
_____

7.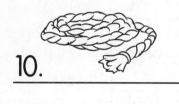
_____
- - - - - - - - -
_____

8.
_____
- - - - - - - - -
_____

9.
_____
- - - - - - - - -
_____

10.
_____
- - - - - - - - -
_____

11.
_____
- - - - - - - - -
_____

12.
_____
- - - - - - - - -
_____

Name_____ Date_____

Read each sentence. Circle the word that best completes the sentence. Write the word on the line.

_____ _ _ _ _ _ _ _ _ _ 1. We will _____ to the store.	**no** **go** **so**
_____ _ _ _ _ _ _ _ _ _ 2. Did the wind _____ the tree down?	**mow** **blow** **throw**
_____ _ _ _ _ _ _ _ _ _ 3. I like to sleep in my _____ bed.	**own** **blown** **grown**
_____ _ _ _ _ _ _ _ _ _ 4. I _____ we can play outside today.	**nose** **hope** **slow**
_____ _ _ _ _ _ _ _ _ _ 5. _____ crayons belong to Joan.	**Those** **Post** **Toe**
_____ _ _ _ _ _ _ _ _ _ 6. I want to be a _____ for Halloween.	**grown** **glow** **ghost**
_____ _ _ _ _ _ _ _ _ _ 7. Mom _____ us to the baseball game.	**vote** **snow** **drove**

Unit 3

Long Vowel e (1)

Name_____ Date_____

The word **leaf** has the **long e** sound.

l<u>ea</u>f

Say the name of each picture. Color the pictures in each row that have the **long e** sound.

1.

2.

3.

4.

5.

Name_____ Date _____

The word **feet** has the **long e** sound. f<u>ee</u>t

Say the name of each picture. Circle the word that names the picture.

1. 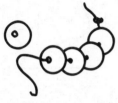	2. 	3. 
bunk **bead**	**peel** **pet**	**read** **red**
4. 	5. 	6.
puppy **peach**	**meal** **melt**	**queen** **quick**
7. 	8. 	9. 
jeep **jump**	**shirt** **sheep**	**loaf** **leaf**
10. 	11. 	12.
smell **seal**	**meat** **mile**	**seat** **sell**

Name_____ Date _____

Say the name of each picture.
Write a word for the second picture that rhymes.

1.

_____   _____

sea

2.

_____   _____

beet

3.

_____   _____

tree

4.

_____   _____

beach

5.

_____   _____

meal

6.

_____   _____

heel

Long Vowel e (IV)

Name_____ Date_____

Read the words.
Write a word from the box to complete each sentence.

clean	dream	knee	seed	she	tea

1. We drank _____ and ate cookies at the party.

2. The boy had a scary _____ .

3. _____ is my best friend.

4. I hurt my _____ while riding my bike.

5. The tiny _____ grew into a giant beanstalk!

6. I will help Dad _____ the garage.

Name_____ Date_____

The letter **y** in **bunny**  makes the **long e** sound.

The letter **y** in **fly**  makes the **long i** sound.

Say each picture name. If it ends like **bunny**, write an **e** on the line. If it ends like **fly**, write an **i** on the line.

1. **pony**
_____
- - - - - - - - -
_____

2. **sky**
_____
- - - - - - - - -
_____

3. **dry**
_____
- - - - - - - - -
_____

4. **funny**
_____
- - - - - - - - -
_____

5. **cry**
_____
- - - - - - - - -
_____

6. **city**
_____
- - - - - - - - -
_____

7. **family**
_____
- - - - - - - - -
_____

8. **happy**
_____
- - - - - - - - -
_____

9. **fry**
_____
- - - - - - - - -
_____

Name_____ Date _____

Read each sentence. Circle the word that best completes
the sentence. Write the word on the line.

_____ - - - - - - - - - - - - 1. My _____ is big.	**funny** **family** **fussy**
_____ - - - - - - - - - 2. The _____ is pretty.	**sky** **shy** **sly**
_____ - - - - - - - - - 3. Did you _____ the wet dish?	**doll** **dry** **by**
_____ - - - - - - - - 4. It is _____ to fry an egg.	**easy** **each** **dizzy**
_____ - - - - - - - - - - - 5. The plant is _____ dry.	**hairy** **ready** **very**
_____ - - - - - - 6. _____ is he sleepy?	**Why** **Try** **Fly**
_____ - - - - - - - - - - - - - 7. The silly puppy has _____ paws.	**spy** **muddy** **merry**

Name_____ Date _____

Fill in the circle next to each word in the row
that has the same vowel sound.

1.

Long a

○ snail   ○ tape   ○ coat   ○ vase

2.

Long e

○pea   ○pie   ○seal   ○meat

3.

Long i

○ kite   ○ pine   ○ fly   ○ fish

4.

Long o

○ bone   ○ rope   ○ log   ○ boat

5.

Long u

○ tub   ○ mule   ○ cube   ○ suit

Name_____ Date_____

Say the name of each picture.
Fill in the circle next to the word that names the picture.

1.

○ wag
○ what
○ whale

2.

○ then
○ tent
○ ten

3.

○ smell
○ smile
○ smoke

4.

○ mill
○ mole
○ mule

5.

○ step
○ stop
○ stove

6.

○ hat
○ hay
○ hail

7.

○ jeep
○ jet
○ jam

8.

○ tea
○ tie
○ try

9.

○ flag
○ fig
○ frog

10.

○ skate
○ swim
○ swing

11.

○ track
○ truck
○ train

12.

○ violin
○ very
○ van

R Blends (1)

Read the words. Notice the sound that the two letters at the beginning of each word make.

drum    **fr**og    **gr**apes

 **cr**ab    **br**ick   **pr**ize   **tr**ee

Color the pictures in each row that have the same beginning sound as the first picture.

1.				
2.				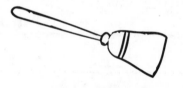
3.				
4.				
5.				

R Blends (II)

Name_____ Date_____

Read the words in the box.
Write the correct word from the box to name each picture.

bride	bridge	brush	crab	crib	drill
drip	frame	frog	grapes	pretzel	tree

1.
_____

2.
_____

3.
_____

4.
_____

5.
_____

6.
_____

7. _____

8.
_____

9. _____

10. _____

11. _____

12. _____

Name_____ Date_____

 **fl**ower  **bl**ock  **cl**oud  **pl**ug   **gl**ass  **sl**eeve

Color the pictures in each row that have the same beginning sound as the first picture.

1.

2.

3.

4.

L Blends (II)

Name_____ Date_____

Read the words in the box.
Write the correct word from the box to name each picture.

blanket	**block**	**clip**	**clue**	**flag**	**flower**
glove	**glue**	**plant**	**plate**	**slate**	**slip**

1.
_____

2.
_____

3.
_____

4.
_____

5.
_____

6.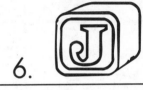
_____

7.
_____

8.
_____

9.
_____

10.
_____

11.
_____

12.
_____

Name_____ Date_____

smile   **sn**ake   **st**ool   **sp**ill   **sw**im   **sk**ate

Say the name of each picture.
Circle the letters the stand for the beginning sound.

1. 	2. 	3. 	4.
sp **sw**	**sm** **sp**	**sn** **st**	**sn** **sp**

5. 	6. 	7.	8. 
sp **st**	**st** **sw**	**sw** **sm**	**sn** **sw**

9. 	10. 	11. 	12. 
sn **sp**	**sn** **sw**	**sp** **st**	**sm** **sn**

13. 	14. 	15. 	16. 
sk **st**	**sw** **sk**	**sp** **st**	**st** **sc**

Name_____ Date_____

Read the words in the box. Say the name of each picture.
Write the word from the box that names the picture.

skate	smile	snail	snake	sniff	spell
stamp	stick	stir	swan	swim	swing

1.
_____

2.
_____

3.
_____

4.
_____

5.
_____

6.
_____

7.
_____

8.
_____

9.
_____

10.
_____

11.
_____

12.
_____

Name_____ Date_____

Say the name of each picture.
Circle the letters that stand for the ending sound.

1.	2.	3.	4.
nt ck	ng nd	nt ck	nd ng

5.	6.	7.	8.
ck ng	nt ck	nt ng	nd ng

9.	10.	11.	12.
ng ck	nd ng	nd ng	ck ng

13.	14.	15.	16.
nt ck	ck sk	nd nt	ck nt

17.	18.	19.	20.
st sp	nd mp	sk ck	sk nt

Name_____ Date_____

Say the name of each picture.
Fill in the circle next to the word that names the picture.

1.
○ clap
○ drop
○ tree

2.
○ glove
○ grab
○ flap

3.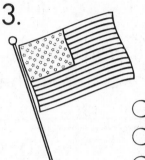
○ play
○ drip
○ flag

4.
○ stop
○ spoon
○ snail

5.
○ truck
○ clip
○ drum

6.
○ star
○ skip
○ sweet

7.
○ prize
○ drive
○ cloud

8.
○ broom
○ trip
○ glue

9.
○ grill
○ floor
○ crib

10.
○ plant
○ glad
○ sled

11.
○ print
○ block
○ price

12.
○ step
○ smell
○ swing

Beginning and Ending th

Name_____ Date_____

The beginning sound in **thirteen** 13 is spelled **th**.

The ending sound in **moth** is spelled **th**.

Read the words in the box.
Write a word from the box to complete each sentence.

bath	path	thorn	three	tooth

1. The cat has a _____ stuck in its paw.

2. My little brother is _____ years old.

3. It is time to take a _____ .

4. Beth has a loose _____ .

5. We walked on the _____ in the park.

Name_____ Date_____

The beginning sound in **wheel** is spelled **wh**.

wheel

Read the words in the box.
Write a word from the box to complete each sentence.

whale	What	wheat	When	Where

1. The farmer grew _____ on his farm.

2. _____ time is my ballet practice?

3. A _____ is a mammal.

4. _____ is my book?

5. _____ will Dad be home?

Name_____ Date_____

The beginning sound in **shoe** is spelled **sh**.

The ending sound in **dish** is spelled **sh**.

Read the words in the box.
Write a word from the box to complete each sentence.

brush	bush	shine	shovel	trash

1. Use a _____ to dig the hole.

2. Grandma planted a _____ between the trees.

3. My job is to take out the _____.

4. The stars _____ so bright at night.

5. My sister likes to _____ her long hair.

Name_____ Date_____

The beginning sound in **chair** is spelled **ch**.

The ending sound in **branch** 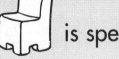 is spelled **ch**.

Read the words in the box.
Write a word from the box to complete each sentence.

bench	cheese	chicken	chop	inch

1. I helped my Dad _____ wood.

2. Do you like _____ on your hamburger?

3. The man sat on the _____ and rested.

4. I grew an _____ this year!

5. The _____ laid an egg.

Unit 4

Digraph kn

Name_____ Date_____

The beginning sound in **knot** is spelled **kn**.

knot

- -

Read the words in the box.
Write a word from the box to complete each sentence.

| knee   knew   knight   knit   knock |

_____
- - - - - - - - - - - - -

1. Did you hear the _____ at the door?

_____
- - - - - - - - - - - - -

2. I scraped my _____ while rollerblading.

_____
- - - - - - - - - - - - -

3. The brave _____ saved the princess.

_____
- - - - - - - - - - - - -

4. I _____ all the answers yesterday.

_____
- - - - - - - - - - - - -

5. Grandma will _____ the baby a hat.

Digraph Practice

Say the name of each picture.
Fill in the circle next to the word that names the picture.

1.

○ cheese
○ shell
○ thick

2.

○ check
○ shed
○ whale

3.

○ chip
○ shop
○ thumb

4.

○ check
○ shack
○ thin

5.

○ chick
○ shark
○ what

6.
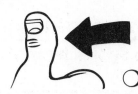
○ chin
○ shell
○ wheel

7.

○ bath
○ bench
○ bush

8.

○ fast
○ fish
○ five

9.

○ bat
○ bath
○ beach

10.
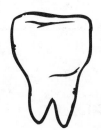
○ tent
○ thin
○ tooth

11.

○ brush
○ buck
○ show

12.

○ wand
○ watch
○ wish

Unit 4

Name_____ Date_____

Read each sentence. Add **-ed** to the word below the blank and write the new word to complete the sentence.

_____
- - - - - - - - - - - -
1. Our family _____ hard today.
   (work)

_____
- - - - - - - - - - - -
2. Sally _____ the gate.
   (fix)

_____
- - - - - - - - - - - -
3. Ted _____ the van.
   (wash)

_____
- - - - - - - - - - - -
4. Bobby _____ the grass.
   (mow)

_____
- - - - - - - - - - - -
5. Sara _____ flowers in the garden.
   (plant)

_____
- - - - - - - - - - - -
6. Then we all _____.
   (rest)

Name_____ Date_____

Read each sentence. Add **-ing** to the word below the blank and write the new word to complete the sentence.

_____

1. Carla is _____ the seeds.
   (water)

2. She is _____ for them to sprout.
   (wait)

3. The seeds will be _____ soon.
   (grow)

4. Carla likes _____ the beans.
   (pick)

5. Mom is _____ bean soup.
   (cook)

6. We like _____ Mom's bean soup!
   (eat)

Unit 5

-ed and -ing Ending

Read each sentence. Circle the correct ending for the word under the blank to complete the sentence. Write the new word.

1. Mom _____ Ann's toy.
   (fix)

   ed
   ing

2. My teacher _____ me with my math.
   (help)

   ed
   ing

3. Lisa is _____ a dog.
   (draw)

   ed
   ing

4. Pat is _____ up the hill.
   (walk)

   ed
   ing

5. It _____ all day.
   (rain)

   ed
   ing

6. The pups are _____.
   (bark)

   ed
   ing

Name_____ Date_____

Read the words in the box.
Write a word from the box to complete each sentence.

after	brown	did	find	from	give	help
know	made	round	soon	that	under	your

1. I got a letter _____ my friend.

2. I _____ a vase out of clay.

3. Is that _____ cup of milk or mine?

4. I found my socks _____ my bed.

5. Pretty _____ we will go to the show.

6. Joe likes to _____ Dad fix the car.

Unit 5

Name_____ Date_____

Unscramble the letters to make a word.
Use the words at the bottom if you need help.

1. newt _____

2. tawh _____

3. nfid _____

4. nmya _____

5. own _____

6. agnia _____

7. eewr _____

8. hten _____

9. umch _____

10. cmoe _____

11. csabeeu _____

12. ervo _____

13. eliv _____

14. wnhe _____

now	then	find	when	what	over	were	live
went	many	come	again	much	because		

Spelling

Name_____ Date_____

Fill in the circle next to the word that is spelled correctly.

1.
- ○ thay
- ○ they
- ○ thae

2.
- ○ get
- ○ git
- ○ jit

3.
- ○ wat
- ○ whut
- ○ what

4.
- ○ frst
- ○ first
- ○ furst

5.
- ○ was
- ○ wuz
- ○ wus

6.
- ○ sed
- ○ said
- ○ sede

7.
- ○ have
- ○ hav
- ○ hafe

8.
- ○ wunt
- ○ want
- ○ whant

9.
- ○ thr
- ○ thir
- ○ there

10.
- ○ wif
- ○ with
- ○ weth

11.
- ○ again
- ○ agin
- ○ agane

12.
- ○ does
- ○ doz
- ○ duz

13.
- ○ liek
- ○ like
- ○ lik

14.
- ○ wunt
- ○ whent
- ○ went

15.
- ○ some
- ○ sume
- ○ som

16.
- ○ relle
- ○ really
- ○ reale

17.
- ○ come
- ○ cume
- ○ com

18.
- ○ mi
- ○ mie
- ○ my

19.
- ○ ar
- ○ are
- ○ ary

20.
- ○ wak
- ○ walk
- ○ walck

Unit 5

Alphabetical Order

Name_____ Date_____

a b c d e f g h i j k l m n o p
q r s t u v w x y z

Read the words in each group.
Number the words **1**, **2**, and **3** to put them in alphabetical order.

1.
___ red
___ blue
___ yellow

2.
___ mouse
___ tiger
___ bear

3.
___ plane
___ car
___ boat

4.
___ Dad
___ Sister
___ Mom

5.
___ soccer
___ football
___ baseball

6.
___ run
___ jog
___ walk

7.
___ grapes
___ banana
___ apple

8.
___ play
___ game
___ fun

9.
___ moon
___ star
___ planet

10.
___ basket
___ doll
___ wagon

11.
___ yak
___ zebra
___ turtle

12.
___ skateboard
___ bike
___ rollerblades

13.
___ tree
___ bush
___ flower

14.
___ hot dog
___ pizza
___ taco

15.
___ ice
___ snow
___ boots

16.
___ desk
___ teacher
___ pencil

Compound Words (1)

Name_____ Date_____

A **compound word** is made from two or more shorter words.

 + = **starfish**

| butterfly | football | handbag | mailbox | pancake | raincoat |

Say the name of each picture. Put the names together to make a compound word. Write the new word.

1.  + = _____

2. + = _____

3.  + = _____

4. + = _____

5. + = _____

6.  + 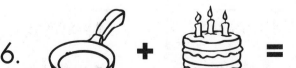 = _____

 Unit 5

Compound Words (II)

Name_____ Date_____

Say the name of each picture. Put the names together to make a compound word. Write the new word.

1. snow + man = _____

2. pin + wheel = _____

3. tea + pot = _____

4. cup + cake = _____

5. dog + house = _____

6. star + fish = _____

Name_____ Date_____

Read the words in the box.
Write a word from the box to complete each sentence.

again	because	come	cupcake	sandbox	were

_____

1. We can't go outside _____ it's raining.

_____

2. Please _____ to my party.

_____

3. Where _____ you yesterday?

_____

4. May I eat a _____ for dessert?

_____

5. Can we play that game _____?

_____

6. Julie made a castle in the _____.

Contractions (I)

Name_____ Date_____

A contraction is a way of putting two words together and making them shorter. **do + not = don't** **Do not** go in my room. **Don't** go in my room.	Sometimes the first word changes. **will + not = won't** I **will not** go in your room. I **won't** go in your room.

Read the contractions. Write the contraction that can be used in place of each pair of words.

aren't	can't	didn't	doesn't	don't
hasn't	**haven't**	**isn't**	**weren't**	**won't**

1. did not _____

2. has not _____

3. can not _____

4. were not _____

5. have not _____

6. is not _____

7. will not _____

8. are not _____

9. do not _____

10. does not _____

Contractions (II)

Read the first sentence.
Write the correct contraction to complete the second sentence.

We are going to the beach!

- -

1. _____ going to the beach!

They are in the water.

- -

2. _____ in the water.

You are late for lunch.

- -

3. _____ late for lunch.

You are reading!

- -

4. _____ reading!

We are going to the movies.

- -

5. _____ going to the movies.

They are riding their bikes.

- -

6. _____ riding their bikes.

Unit 5

Contractions (III)

Name_____ Date_____

A contraction is a way of putting two words together and making them shorter.	I + will = I'll **I will** eat my lunch. **I'll** eat my lunch.

Read the contractions.
Write the two words that make up each contraction.

1. we'll _____   _____

2. they'll _____   _____

3. he'll _____   _____

4. I'll _____   _____

5. it'll _____   _____

6. you'll _____   _____

7. who'll _____   _____

Contractions (IV)

| she is = she's | it is = it's | he is = he's. |

Read the sentences.
Write a contraction to replace each group of underlined words.

It is a nice day to go to the zoo.

_ _ _ _ _ _ _ _ _ _ _ _ _ _ _ _ _ _ _

1. _____ a nice day to go the zoo.

She is watching the polar bears.

_ _ _ _ _ _ _ _ _ _ _ _ _ _ _ _ _ _ _

2. _____ watching the polar bears.

He is feeding the sea lions.

_ _ _ _ _ _ _ _ _ _ _ _ _ _ _

3. _____ feeding the sea lions.

He is talking to the parrots.

_ _ _ _ _ _ _ _ _ _ _ _ _ _ _

4. _____ talking to the parrots.

It is hot. Let's get some ice cream!

_ _ _ _ _ _ _ _ _ _ _ _ _ _ _ _ _

5. _____ hot. Let's get some ice cream!

Unit 5

Contraction Practice

Read the contractions in the box. Write a contraction from the box to replace each group of underlined words.

can't	I'm	I'll	She's	We're	You'll

1. _____ going to a farm.
   <u>We are</u>

2. _____ ride a pony.
   <u>You will</u>

3. _____ going for a ride on the tractor.
   <u>I am</u>

4. _____ feed the goats.
   <u>I will</u>

5. _____ chasing the chickens.
   <u>She is</u>

6. We _____ jump in the haystack.
   <u>can not</u>

Synonyms

Words with the same or almost the same meaning are called **synonyms**.

Close and **shut** are synonyms.

Read the first word in each row. Circle the synonym.

1.	car	bike	auto	plow
2.	small	little	big	huge
3.	build	hammer	make	ladder
4.	big	tiny	dog	large
5.	yell	talk	shout	girl
6.	night	evening	day	moon
7.	look	sleep	see	jump
8.	fast	run	slow	quick

Unit 5

Antonyms

Antonyms are words with opposite meanings.
New and **old** are antonyms.

new     old

Read the first word in each row. Circle the antonym.

1.	over	up	jog	under
2.	full	big	empty	take
3.	fat	thin	tall	old
4.	big	large	sun	little
5.	strong	sad	weak	cry
6.	in	door	come	out
7.	dry	wet	hot	wash
8.	hot	cook	cold	fire

Adjectives

Name_____ Date_____

Adjectives tell more about nouns.
They can answer these questions:

What kind?
fuzzy bears

How many?
two bears

What color?
brown bears

- -

Read each sentence.
Circle the correct adjective and write it to complete the sentence.

1. This is a _____ flower.
   pretty   grow

2. I see _____ mice.
   bug   tiny

3. She has _____ hair.
   long   smile

4. The _____ bus is red.
   big   tires

5. The _____ birds sing.
   black   beak

6. His mitt is _____ .
   new   up

7. He has _____ sisters.
   fire   four

6. The dogs are _____ .
   tail   small

Unit 5

Name_____ Date_____

Read the words in the box.
Write a word from the box to answer each riddle.

back crispy day down five hop long unhappy

1. I am the opposite of front. _____

2. I mean the same as sad. _____

3. I am the kind of pizza crust you have. _____

4. I am the opposite of short. _____

5. I mean the same as jump. _____

6. I can tell how many fingers you have. _____

7. I am the opposite of up. _____

8. I am the opposite of night. _____

Name_____ Date_____

The pictures in each row tell a story, but they are out of order. Write **1** by the event that-happened first, **2** by the event that happened-next, and **3** by the event that happened last.

1.

2.

3.

Name_____ Date_____

These pictures tell a story, but they are out of order.
Number them from **1** to **6** to show the order of what happened.

Main Idea (I)

The **main idea** of a story is its most important part.

Each group of pictures tells a story.
Look the pictures and circle the sentence that tells the main idea.

1.

The birthday party was fun.   Jason got a bike for his birthday.

Noone had fun at the party.   Jason's cake was big.

2.

Sue gave away three kittens.   Sue does not like kittens.

Sue kept all the kittens.   The kittens were gray.

Unit 6

Main Idea (II)

Name_____ Date_____

Read each story.
Fill in the circle next to the sentence that tells the main idea.

1. Tracy sees that it is raining. She puts on boots. She puts on a raincoat. She puts on a hat. Now she is ready.

   ○ **Tracy dresses for a rainy day.**
   ○ **Tracy takes a long time to get ready.**

2. Paint is coming off the old house. The windows are broken. The front door is loose. The roof has big holes.

   ○ **The old house is nice.**
   ○ **The old house needs to be fixed.**

3. Joey had a good day. He found a dime on the ground. He got an A on his work. A friend chose him for her team. His mom gave him a big hug.

   ○ **Joey has lots of friends.**
   ○ **Joey had a good day.**

Name_____ Date_____

Read the story. Then, fill in the story map.

It is easy to make a cheese sandwich. First, spread butter on two slices of bread. Next, put some cheese between the bread slices. Cut the sandwich in half. Now it is ready to eat!

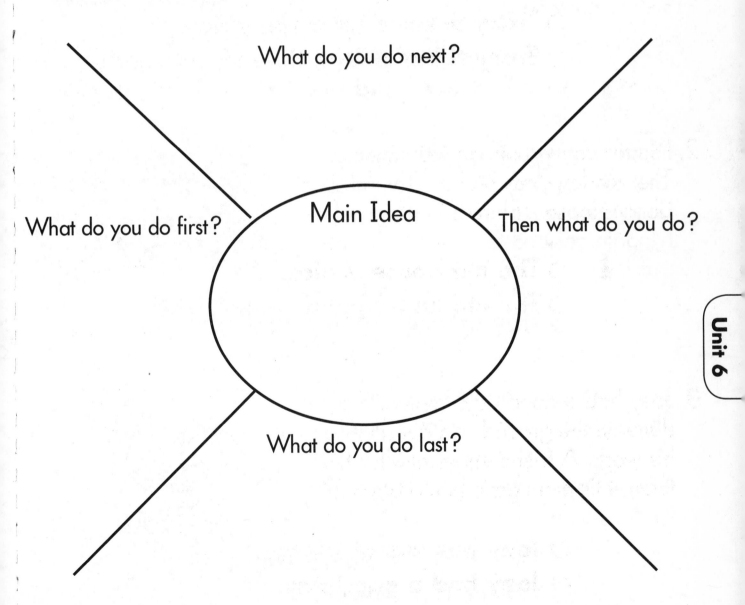

What do you do next?

What do you do first?

Main Idea

Then what do you do?

What do you do last?

Predicting Outcomes

Name_____ Date_____

Read each story beginning. Then, fill in the circle next to the sentence ending that makes the most sense.

1. Brendon woke up excited and happy. The sun was shining. It was a perfect day for a trip to the beach. After a few seconds, Brendon

   ○ **jumped out of bed.**
   ○ **rolled over and went back to sleep.**

2. Maggie knew a storm was coming. The sky was gray. A strong wind began to blow. Thunder rolled. Maggie decided to

   ○ **go outside and play.**
   ○ **stay inside with her family.**

3. Dee was ready for the dance show. She had done her steps over and over. Before the show, she felt sure of herself. She smiled as she came onto the stage. Then Dee

   ○ **forgot all the dance steps.**
   ○ **did the dance well.**

Name_____ Date_____

Look for clues in each picture. Circle the sentence that tells what most likely happened between the two pictures in each row.

1. The girl threw the ball at the window.

The girl batted the ball through the window.

Someone in the house broke the window.

2. The sun came out.

It got colder.

Someone pushed the snowman over.

Unit 6

3. The boy sawed the branch off.

Lightning struck the tree.

The branch broke off.

Inferences

Name_____ Date_____

Use the picture clues to guess what is happening.
Circle the guess that fits the clues.

1. This boy just won a race.

   This boy just lost a race.

2.  The show is about to begin.

   The show is done.

3. It is very quiet.

   The girl hears loud noises.

4.  Sam just ate a jelly sandwich.

   Sam has not eaten all day.

5. This girl likes carrots.

   This girl does not like carrots.

6. Today is windy.

   There is no wind today.

Name_____ Date_____

Read Joy's story. Then, fill in the circle next to the correct answer.

Our family went to town to see the parade. At about noon, we joined a big crowd. My brother Roy was in the band. Dad pointed out where he was. We could all see him and we shouted and waved. The band music sounded good and loud.

The parade lasted about a half an hour. We all enjoyed it. If I had my choice, I would see a parade every day.

1. What is the main idea of the story?
   - ○ The band music was loud.
   - ○ Joy's family waved to Dad.
   - ○ Joy's family saw a parade.

2. Where did Joy's family go to see the parade?
   - ○ in town
   - ○ to school
   - ○ to a football game

3. What did Joy have to say about the band music?
   - ○ It was bad.
   - ○ The drums were too loud.
   - ○ It was good and loud.

4. What do you think the family will do the next time there is a parade?
   - ○ They will stay home.
   - ○ They will go to the parade.
   - ○ They will go to the zoo.

Unit 6

Name_____ Date_____

Read the story. Then, fill in the circle next to the correct answer.

It is fun to shop in the city. Mom and I get on the bus at Oak Street. First, we pass the school. Then, the bus takes us over a bridge. Soon, we see a tall building with a red flag. We pass lots of people walking. At Main Street, the bus driver stops the bus and Mom and I step off. Now it is time to shop!

1. What is the main idea of the story?
   ○ We see tall buildings.
   ○ We ride the bus.
   ○ Mom and I shop in the city.

2. What do Mom and I pass first?
   ○ the school
   ○ lots of people
   ○ our home

3. Where does the bus stop?
   ○ at the building
   ○ at the school
   ○ at Main Street

4. What do you think will happen next?
   ○ Mom and I will go back home.
   ○ Mom and I will go shopping.
   ○ Mom and I will visit Grandma.

Capitalization (1)

Name_____ Date_____

The first word in a sentence always begins with a **capital letter**.

The boys like to play catch.

↖ capital letter

Read each sentence. Fill in the circle next to the sentences that begin with a capital letter.

○ 1. That little mouse eats cheese.

○ 2. my Dad is fixing the car.

○ 3. Did you see the movie?

○ 4. I got a new bike for my birthday.

○ 5. he is playing with his truck.

○ 6. when will we go to the park?

○ 7. My dog likes to bark at the mailman.

○ 8. The teacher passed out the papers.

○ 9. the boat is on the lake.

○ 10. Julie will help bake cookies.

Unit 7

Name_____ Date_____

Underline the word that should be capitalized in each sentence. Then, rewrite the sentence correctly.

1. the baby is sleeping.

_____

_____

2. we are going to the park.

_____

_____

3. mom is cooking fish.

_____

_____

4. i am having a party.

_____

_____

5. a bee stung me.

_____

_____

6. today is a great day.

_____

_____

Punctuation (I)

Name_____ Date_____

A sentence that tells something ends with a **period**.
It is called a **statement**.

My dog is black and white.

period →

- -

Read each sentence.
Fill in the circle next to the sentence that is written correctly.

○ 1. The boat can sail on the lake

○ 2. It is good to drink a lot of water.

○ 3. Today we played outside.

○ 4. I will help Dad rake the leaves.

○ 5. Patrick is my best friend

○ 6. The turtle sat on a rock.

○ 7. The cat naps on my bed

○ 8. Tyler gave his Mom a hug

○ 9. We watched a movie last night.

○ 10. Grandma read me a story.

Unit 7

Punctuation (II)

Name_____ Date_____

Read each sentence. If it needs a period, add it.
Then, rewrite the sentence correctly.

1. The sky is blue

_____

_____

2. Our team won the game.

_____

3. The puppy chewed my shoe.

_____

4. It is fun to fly a kite

_____

_____

5. Please close the door.

_____

_____

6. I like to paint

_____

Punctuation (III)

Name_____ Date_____

A sentence that asks a **question** ends with a **question mark**.

Can you kick the ball**?**

↗
question mark

Read each sentence.
Fill in the circle next to each sentence that asks a question.

○ 1. It will rain today.

○ 2. What is your name?

○ 3. I think he is at the door.

○ 4. Who won the game?

○ 5. He doesn't know your brother.

○ 6. Can I use your pencil?

○ 7. What time is it?

○ 8. You did not watch the video.

○ 9. Kangaroos live in Australia.

○ 10. Would you like an apple or an orange?

Unit 7

Punctuation (IV)

Name_____ Date_____

Read each sentence. If it needs a question mark, add it.
Then, rewrite the sentence correctly.

1. May I go with you

_____

_____

2. How old are you?

_____

_____

3. What are you doing

_____

_____

4. Do you know how to get there?

_____

_____

5. Are you leaving now?

_____

_____

6. What is your favorite movie

_____

Punctuation (V)

Name_____ Date_____

A sentence that shows **excitement** ends with an **exclamation point**.

Run**!**

exclamation point

Read each sentence.
Fill in the circle next to each sentence that shows excitement.

○ 1. Joshua can run one mile.

○ 2. Did you read that book?

○ 3. Watch out!

○ 4. Lindsey needs to clean her room.

○ 5. Ouch!

○ 6. That was a great game!

○ 7. This soup is hot!

○ 8. Can we play in the snow?

○ 9. Wow! You did a great job!

○ 10. It is very windy in Chicago.

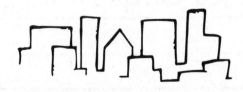

Unit 7

Name_____ Date_____

Rewrite each sentence using the correct capitalization and punctuation.

1. my favorite color is blue

_____

_____

2. can we watch a video

_____

_____

3. wow that building is tall

_____

_____

4. i am so hungry

_____

_____

5. dad is taking us to the park

_____

_____

6. are you feeling ill

_____

_____

Nouns

Name_____ Date_____

A word that names a person, place, or thing is called a **noun**.

 mother
person

 home
place

 purse
thing

Read the words in the box.
Write the correct word from the box to name each picture.

| barn bug car city farmer flower girl hat shop |

1.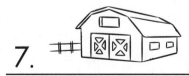
_____

2.
_____

3.
_____

4.
_____

5.
_____

6.
_____

7.
_____

8.
_____

9.
_____

Unit 7

Proper Nouns

A **proper noun** is the name of an exact person, place, or thing. Every **proper noun** begins with a capital letter.

United **S**tates   **J**une

Read each sentence and circle the proper noun that is not written correctly. Rewrite the proper noun correctly.

1. The train goes to boston. _____

2. I live on park road. _____

3. maria ran home fast. _____

4. Her birthday is in march. _____

5. That man lives in japan. _____

6. ken rides a red bike. _____

Name_____ Date_____

To make many nouns mean "more than one" add **s** at the end.
Adding **s** makes a plural noun.

one bear

three bear**s**

Read each word in the box. If the word is plural, write it on the
Animals list. If the word is not plural, write it on the **Animal** list.

birds   cats   dogs   ducks   frog   horse   lion   pig   rabbits   tiger

Animal	**Animals**
_____	_____
_____	_____
_____	_____
_____	_____
_____	_____
_____	_____

Unit 7

Plural Nouns (II)

Name_____ Date_____

A **plural noun** names "more than one."
Add **-es** to a noun ending in **s**, **x**, **ch**, or **sh** to make it **plural**.

one dress   two dress**es**   one fox   two fox**es**

- -

Rewrite each noun, adding **-es** to make it plural.

1. match _____

2. bus _____

3. brush _____

4. box _____

5. six _____

6. inch _____

7. glass _____

8. wish _____

Verbs (1)

Name_____ Date_____

A **verb** is a word that tells what a person or thing does.

The sun **shines**.

Circle the verb in each sentence.

1. Boats sail on the sea.

2. We run on the sandy beach.

3. A woman sits in the sun.

4. Our ice cream melts.

5. Waves come to the shore.

6. The girls play a game.

7. The boy throws a ball.

8. Dad dives into the water.

Unit 7

Verbs (II)

Name_____ Date_____

A **verb** usually ends in **s** when it tells about only one person or thing. A **verb** usually does not end in **s** when it tells about more than one person or thing.

The star **twinkle<u>s</u>**.　　　　　　　Stars **twinkle**.

Read each sentence. Circle the correct verb to complete it.

1. The little bear_____ a spacesuit.
    wear   wears

2. Bears _____ into space today.
    go   goes

3. The bears _____ into the spaceship.
    get   gets

4. The big bear _____ pictures.
    take   takes

5. The little bear _____ into space.
    float   floats

6. The bears _____ at the planets.
    look   looks

Verbs (III)

Choose the correct verb to complete each sentence. Write the verb.

_____

1. Tina _____ to the park.
   walks   walking

_____

2. Our class _____ the museum.
   visit   visited

_____

3. Jim _____ the TV show.
   watch   watches

_____

4. Mom is _____ the dishes.
   washed   washing

_____

5. Some children are _____ a picture.
   paint   painting

_____

6. The kitten _____ when its happy.
   purrs   purring

Unit 7

Writing Sentences

Name_____ Date_____

Every sentence has two parts. The **naming part** is who or what is being talked about. The **action part** tells what a person or thing does or is.

The cat   plays with yarn.

naming part   action part

Draw a line to match each naming part with an action part.

Naming Parts	**Action Parts**
The toy car	is open late.
The girls	bark loudly.
Snow	is tall.
My father	is falling on the tree.
The dogs	is broken.
That store	are best friends.

Write two of the sentences you made.

1. _____

2. _____

Recognizing Sentences

Name_____ Date_____

Does the sentence make sense? Circle **Yes** or **No**.

1. A house can jump.   Yes   No

2. I can hide in a house.   Yes   No

3. A bus can hide.   Yes   No

4. I can push a store.   Yes   No

5. I can ride a bike in a park.   Yes   No

6. I can paste a bike on a park.   Yes   No

7. A car can go.   Yes   No

8. A car can stop.   Yes   No

9. The boy can rake a train.   Yes   No

10. Mom likes to bake pies.   Yes   No

Unit 7

Word Order

Unscramble the words to make a complete sentence. Write the sentence.

1. is in frog the A pond.

_____

_____

2. movie funny The was.

_____

_____

3. catch I play Dad and.

_____

_____

4. computer Brian can play games.

_____

_____

5. flies windy He kite a day on a.

_____

_____

6. a card mom I for made my.

_____

_____

Noun and Verb Practice

Name_____ Date_____

Write a noun or verb from the box to complete each sentence.

ape	ball	bear	made	went	were

_____verb_____

– – – – – – – – – – – – –

1. We _____ to the zoo.

_____noun_____

– – – – – – – – – – – – –

2. I waved to the _____.

_____verb_____

– – – – – – – – – – –

3. The monkeys _____ me laugh.

_____noun_____

– – – – – – – – – – – –

4. The _____ was asleep.

_____verb_____

– – – – – – – – – –

5. The hippos _____ fat.

_____noun_____

– – – – – – – – – –

6. A seal played with a _____.

Unit 7

Name_____ Date_____

Write a naming part for each action part.

1. _____ buried the bone.

2. _____ wore a shiny crown.

3. _____ sold his card collection.

4. _____ climbed up a tree.

Write an action part for each naming part.

5. A butterfly _____.

6. The baby _____.

7. My little sister _____.

Name_____ Date_____

Say the name of the picture at the beginning of each row. Fill in the circle next to the word that has the same **beginning sound** in that row.

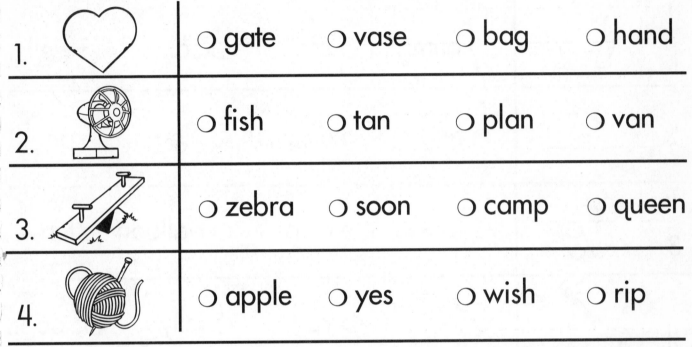

1.	○ gate	○ vase	○ bag	○ hand
2.	○ fish	○ tan	○ plan	○ van
3.	○ zebra	○ soon	○ camp	○ queen
4.	○ apple	○ yes	○ wish	○ rip

Say the name of the picture at the beginning of each row. Fill in the circle next to the word that has the same **ending sound** in that row.

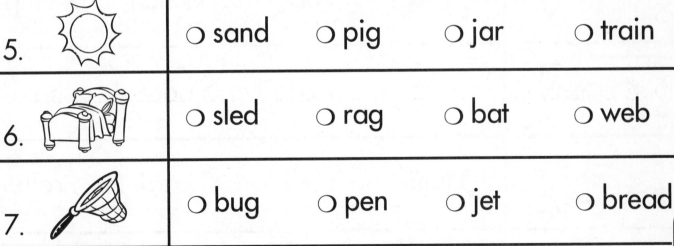

5.	○ sand	○ pig	○ jar	○ train
6.	○ sled	○ rag	○ bat	○ web
7.	○ bug	○ pen	○ jet	○ bread
8.	○ wagon	○ six	○ book	○ frog

Practice Test: Vowels

Name_____ Date_____

Say the name of the picture at the beginning of each row. Fill in the circle next to the word that has the same **vowel sound** in that row.

1.	○ blimp	○ mat	○ cake	○ well
2.	○ fish	○ map	○ then	○ pit
3.	○ top	○ club	○ balloon	○ ten
4.	○ job	○ van	○ jelly	○ spoon
5.	○ like	○ put	○ kitten	○ lump
6.	○ bite	○ lake	○ boat	○ box
7.	○ tune	○ ant	○ yarn	○ rain
8.	○ too	○ seal	○ pet	○ jump

Practice Test: Blends and Digraphs

Name_____ Date_____

Say the name of the picture at the beginning of each row.
Fill in the circle next to the word that has the same **beginning blend** or **digraph** in that row.

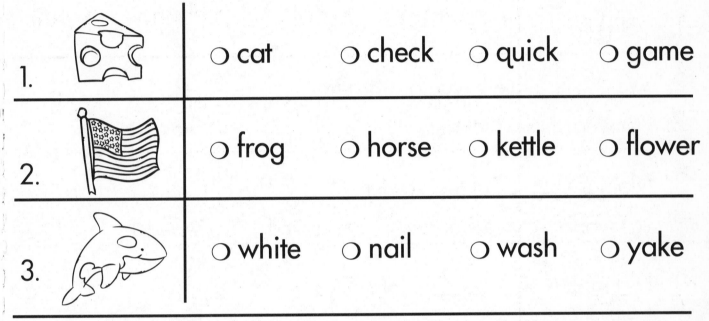

1. ○ cat   ○ check   ○ quick   ○ game

2. ○ frog   ○ horse   ○ kettle   ○ flower

3. ○ white   ○ nail   ○ wash   ○ yake

Say the name of the picture at the beginning of each row.
Fill in the circle next to the word that has the same **ending blend** or **digraph** in that row.

4. ○ block   ○ jam   ○ band   ○ lamb

5. ○ rip   ○ rash   ○ under   ○ glass

6. 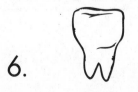 ○ snake   ○ day   ○ moth   ○ boot

Unit 8

Practice Test: Vocabulary

Name_____ Date_____

Read each sentence.
Fill in the circle next to the word that completes the sentence.

1. That gift is _____ my Grandma.

   ○ did   ○ find   ○ from   ○ your

2. We _____ late because of traffic.

   ○ were   ○ what   ○ all   ○ was

3. Mom is _____ in the garden.

   ○ works   ○ working   ○ worked   ○ walked

4. Last night we _____ up late.

   ○ stilled   ○ stayed   ○ staying   ○ started

Fill in the circle next to the word that is spelled correctly.

5. ○ sed   ○ said   ○ sade   ○ sayd

6. ○ more   ○ mur   ○ moore   ○ mor

7. ○ duz   ○ duzz   ○ doz   ○ does

8. ○ whut   ○ what   ○ wat   ○ whaut

Name_____ Date_____

Fill in the circle next to each **compound word**.

1. ○ ticket   ○ umpire   ○ popcorn   ○ jelly

2. ○ ship   ○ outside   ○ other   ○ wait

3. ○ downtown   ○ hello   ○ mother   ○ talk

4. ○ where   ○ seashell   ○ you   ○ tomorrow

5. ○ wrench   ○ turtle   ○ pencil   ○ football

Read the group of words at the beginning of each row. Fill in the circle next to the word that is a **contraction** for that group of words.

6. is not	○ isnot	○ isn't	○ is'nt
7. we are	○ we're	○ won't	○ were
8. you will	○ we'll	○ y'll	○ you'll
9. he is	○ his	○ he's	○ hes'
10. do not	○ don't	○ didn't	○ doesn't

Unit 8

Name_____ Date_____

Say the word at the beginning of each row.
Fill in the circle next to the word in that row that means the **same**.

1. make	○ jump	○ loud	○ build	○ nail
2. big	○ little	○ pickle	○ elephant	○ large
3. yell	○ shout	○ tell	○ brother	○ whisper
4. car	○ bike	○ auto	○ truck	○ bear
5. over	○ right	○ under	○ above	○ see

Say the word at the beginning of each row. Fill in the circle next to the word in that row that means the **opposite**.

6. up	○ little	○ down	○ over	○ ugly
7. small	○ huge	○ boy	○ tiny	○ rock
8. long	○ short	○ big	○ under	○ left
9. morning	○ day	○ night	○ star	○ girl
10. hot	○ up	○ warm	○ mug	○ cold

Name_____ Date_____

Read the paragraphs.
Fill in the circle next to the correct answer to each question.

The city is a noisy place. Cars honk their horns. Brakes squeal. Sirens scream. People call to each other. Music from radios fills the air.

1. What is the main idea?
   ○ There are lots of people in the city.
   ○ The city is noisy.
   ○ The city is not a good place to live.

Mom works hard in her garden. She plants flowers in rows. She pulls weeds. She trims the bushes and sweeps the paths. All her work makes the garden pretty.

2. What does Mom do first in the garden?
   ○ She trims the bushes.
   ○ She pulls weeds.
   ○ She plants flowers.

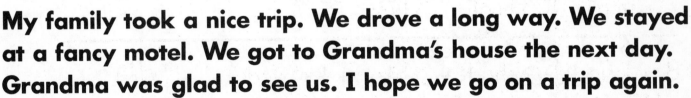

My family took a nice trip. We drove a long way. We stayed at a fancy motel. We got to Grandma's house the next day. Grandma was glad to see us. I hope we go on a trip again.

3. What will most likely happen next?
   ○ Grandma will go on a trip.
   ○ We will have fun visiting Grandma.
   ○ We won't take another trip for a long time.

Unit 8

Name_____ Date_____

Fill in the circle next to the sentence that is written correctly.

1. ○ One day we went to the farm
   ○ it was a great day!
   ○ We saw a lot of animals.

2. ○ My Dad likes to fish.
   ○ He caught a really big one?
   ○ but he had to throw it back in the lake

3. ○ Wow! That was a great roller coaster ride!
   ○ It went really fast
   ○ my little sister screamed.

4. ○ Some day i'd like to visit Texas.
   ○ I heard there is a lot to do
   ○ Where would you like to visit?

5. ○ The busy beaver worked and worked.
   ○ He made a large dam
   ○ Wow? That is a busy beaver.

6. ○ my favorite color is blue?
   ○ Because it is the color of the sky
   ○ What is your favorite color?

7. ○ Are we riding the bus to school?
   ○ the bus picks us up at 8:00.
   ○ i love to ride the bus!

Name_____ Date_____

Fill in the circle next to the word that names a **noun**.

1. ○ jump   ○ hop   ○ flower   ○ pull

2. ○ boy   ○ look   ○ out   ○ sip

Fill in the circle next to the word that names a **verb**.

3. ○ wheel   ○ pig   ○ mother   ○ hop

4. ○ book   ○ turn   ○ green   ○ toy

Fill in the circle next to the word that could describe the noun.

5. _____ boy | ○ radio   ○ tall   ○ box   ○ hut

6. _____ mountain | ○ bus   ○ you   ○ over   ○ snowy

Fill in the circle next to the word that best completes each sentence.

7. Many _____ swim in the pond. | ○ duck   ○ ducks

8. The birds _____ a song. | ○ sing   ○ sings

Unit 8

Practice Test: Sentences

Name_____ Date_____

Fill in the circle next the sentence that makes sense.

1. ○ On Monday, we are going to the museum.
   ○ On Monday, going we to the museum.

2. ○ Do you eat to like pie?
   ○ Do you like to eat pie?

3. ○ My Dad is a trip to Florida taking.
   ○ My Dad is taking a trip to Florida.

Fill in the circle next to the sentence that has the **naming part** underlined.

4. ○ <u>The little boy</u> chased after the rabbit.
   ○ The little boy <u>chased after the rabbit</u>.

5. ○ An airplane <u>flew through the clouds.</u>
   ○ <u>An airplane</u> flew through the clouds.

6. ○ Sara wrote a letter <u>to her friend.</u>
   ○ <u>Sara</u> wrote a letter to her friend.

Fill in the circle next to the sentence that has the **action part** underlined.

7. ○ <u>We</u> watched the sun set.
   ○ We <u>watched the sun set.</u>

8. ○ A green lizard <u>ate a bug.</u>
   ○ <u>A green lizard</u> ate a bug.

9. ○ The baby <u>smiled at me.</u>
   ○ <u>The baby</u> smiled at me.

Answer Key

Page 3
1. saw, sun
2. sailboat, sock
3. six, sink
4. scissors, sandwich
5. soap, seesaw

Page 4
1. tire, telephone
2. top, two
3. TV, tiger
4. ten, tie
5. turtle, table

Page 5
1. bench, bat, balloon
2. boat, baseball, baby
3. bell
4. bird
5. boy
6. bed

Page 6
1. hammer, heart, helicopter
2. house, horn
3. hippo, helmet
4. harp, hen
5. horse, hat

Page 7
1. man   3. milk
4. mice   6. mask
7. moon   9. monkey
10. moose   12. mop
14. motorcycle 15. mitt

Page 8
2. key   4. kite
5. kangaroo 6. kittens
10. kick   11. kettle
15. kitchen

Page 9
1. h   2. t
3. m   4. k
5. b   6. k
7. h   8. s
9. t   10. b
11. s   12. m
13. h   14. t
15. b   16. s

Page 10
1. jar, jack-in-the-box
2. jeep, jacks
3. jump rope, jet
4. jack-o-lantern, jam

Page 11
1. fire, fan
2. fish, five
3. fork, faucet
4. fence, finger

Page 12
2. ghost   4. gate
5. gum   6. goggles
8. guitar
goat, goose

Page 13
1. lamp, lips
2. log, lick
3. lion, ladder
4. lock, leaf

Page 14
2. doll   3. dog
5. dig   6. door
8. doctor   9. duck
12. dinosaur 15. deer

Page 15
2. net   3. nose
5. nail   8. nut
9. needle   10. nurse
13. nickel

Page 16
1. j   2. d
3. f   4. n
5. f   6. l
7. g   8. d
9. j   10. n
11. g   12. l

Page 17
2. watermelon 3. watch
6. web   8. walrus
wig, wagon

Page 18
1. cupcake, corn
2. cow, cap
3. cup, carrot
4. can, cave
5. cook, cactus

Page 19
1. roller skates, robe
2. robot, rocket
3. rake, ring
4. rug, raccoon

Answer Key

Page 20
1. pie, pig
2. piano, pail
3. pillow, pear
4. pencil, pony
5. pin, pail

Page 21
3. quarter
4. quilt
6. question mark
9. queen

Page 22
1. van, vest
2. violin, vase
3. vacuum, vegetables
4. van
5. vest
6. valley
7. vase

Page 23
1. pig
2. cat
3. vest
4. raccoon
5. pie
6. quilt
7. van
8. rug
9. pencil
10. volcano
11. well
12. robot

Page 24
1. yak
2. zero
3. yarn
5. zebra
7. yawn
9. x-ray
10. x-ray
12. zipper

Page 25
1. bag/wig, frog
2. sled/hand, bread
3. dog/log, tag
4. bed/head, bird
5. bug/flag, rug

Page 26
1. n
2. n
3. t
4. t
5. t
6. n
7. n
8. t
9. n
10. n
11. t
12. t
13. n
14. t
15. t
16. n

Page 27
1. fox/ax, fox
2. cup/jeep, mop
3. top/cup, cap
4. six/ox, mix
5. map/nap, lamp

Page 28
1. stem/clam, lamb
2. cub/tub, web
3. jam/ham, thumb
4. club/sub, cab
5. gum/arm, broom

Page 29
1. s
2. r
3. s
4. r
5. k
6. s
7. k
8. r
9. k
10. k
11. r
12. s
13. r
14. k
15. k
16. k

Page 30
1. n
2. t
3. g
4. t
5. d
6. k
7. b
8. m
9. b
10. s
11. x
12. r
13. m
14. g
15. n
16. d
17. r
18. p
19. k
20. p

Page 31
1. cat, hand, can
2. lamp, cap
3. bag, fan
4. bat, man, mat

Page 32
1. cat
2. cap
3. hat
4. can
5. man
6. tag
7. map
8. pan
9. ram
10. clam
11. hand
12. mat
13. van
14. rat
15. fan
16. jam
17. bat
18. bag
19. ham
20. lamp

Page 33
1. cat
2. rat
3. flat
4. sat
5. bat
6. fat

Answer Key

Page 34
1. ran
2. van
3. Dan
4. fan
5. pan
6. man

Page 35
1. six, mitt
2. bib, lid
3. kick, hill
4. pig, wig
5. witch, fish

Page 36
1. pin
2. hill
3. king
4. mix
5. six
6. kick
7. pig
8. mitt
9. lips
10. chin
11. crib
12. witch
13. twig
14. fin
15. wig
16. bib

Page 37
1. spin
2. fin
3. twin
4. win
5. chin
6. pin

Page 38
1. pig
2. jig
3. wig
4. dig
5. twig
6. big

Page 39
1. jug, bug
2. sun, drum
3. cub, sub
4. tub, truck
5. bus, duck

Page 40
1. bug
2. duck
3. cub
4. nut
5. jug
6. rug
7. sun
8. cup
9. tub
10. gum
11. cut
12. drum
13. sub
14. hug
15. thumb
16. cuff

Page 41
1. cub
2. sub
3. tub
4. shrub
5. rub
6. stub

Page 42
1. tug
2. rug
3. plug
4. mug
5. bug
6. hug

Page 43
1. dog, top
2. block, sock
3. doll, mop
4. clock, lock
5. fox, log

Page 44
1. ox
2. box
3. mop
4. lock
5. clock
6. pot
7. top
8. knot
9. pop
10. hop
11. cot
12. jog
13. frog
14. log
15. doll
16. rock

Page 45
1. dog
2. job
3. log
4. frog
5. hog
6. fog

Page 46
1. hop
2. stop
3. shop
4. pop
5. mop
6. drop

Page 47
1. jet, web
2. pen, net
3. hen, pen
4. bed, nest
5. sled, well

Page 48
1. bed
2. leg
3. bell
4. tent
5. belt
6. well
7. twelve
8. net
9. pen
10. nest
11. desk
12. pet
13. dress
14. men
15. jet
16. web

Premium Education Language Arts: Grade 1   153   © Learning Horizons

Answer Key

Page 49
1. pet
2. met
3. jet
4. yet
5. wet
6. bet

Page 50
1. hen
2. ten
3. When
4. pen
5. then
6. Ben

Page 51
1. ten
2. rug
3. six
4. fan
5. pin
6. box
7. log
8. hat
9. pig
10. tub
11. web
12. bed

Page 52
1. pet
2. dig
3. frog
4. van
5. sub
6. When
7. hop

Page 53
1. cape
2. tape
3. pine
4. tube
5. plane, not
6. plan, note

Page 54
1. gate
2. plane
3. rake
4. lake
5. tape
6. snake
7. cake
8. skate
9. cane
10. cave
11. wave
12. cape

Page 55
1. snail
2. pail
3. tail
4. braid
5. sail
6. mail
7. rain
8. nail
9. paint

Page 56
1. hay
2. pay
3. gray
4. day
5. May
6. stay

Page 57
1. rake
2. tray
3. snail
4. wave
5. hay
6. train

Page 58
1. tire, dime
2. dice, five
3. vine, kite
4. pie, bike
5. tie, nine

Page 59
1. five
2. mice
3. slide
4. dive
5. hive
6. pie
7. bike
8. dice
9. kite
10. dime
11. bride
12. price
13. vine
14. tire
15. tie
16. pipe

Page 60
1. kite
2. tie
3. dime
4. hive
5. mice
6. bride

Page 61
1. hike
2. line
3. time
4. wipe
5. bite
6. mine

Page 62
1. mule, glue
2. cube, tube
3. tune, suit
4. flute, juice

Page 63
1. Tuesday
2. tube
3. flute
4. cube
5. clue
6. juice
7. bruise
8. fruit
9. mule
10. tune
11. glue
12. suit

Page 64
1. fruit
2. juice
3. flute
4. bruise
5. tube
6. cruise
7. prune
8. cube
9. suit
10. glue
11. rude
12. clue

Page 65
1. tune
2. June
3. blue
4. mule
5. due
6. true
7. cube

Page 66
1. hoe, nose
2. comb, goat
3. soap, cone
4. boat, bone

Answer Key

Answers

Page 67
1. doe
2. cone
3. note
4. coal
5. globe
6. soap
7. coat
8. home
9. toast
10. toe
11. robe
12. boat

Page 68
1. doze
2. snow
3. rose
4. pole
5. boat
6. cone
7. nose
8. toad
9. hole
10. rope
11. road
12. stove

Page 69
1. go
2. blow
3. own
4. hope
5. Those
6. ghost
7. drove

Page 70
1. bee, jeep
2. feet, tree
3. three, heel
4. sheep, beads
5. seal, leaf

Page 71
1. bead
2. peel
3. read
4. peach
5. meal
6. queen
7. jeep
8. sheep
9. leaf
10. seal
11. meat
12. seat

Page 72
1. pea
2. feet
3. bee
4. peach
5. seal
6. peel

Page 73
1. tea
2. dream
3. She
4. knee
5. seed
6. clean

Page 74
1. e
2. i
3. i
4. e
5. i
6. e
7. e
8. e
9. i

Page 75
1. family
2. sky
3. dry
4. easy
5. very
6. Why
7. muddy

Page 76
1. snail, tape, vase
2. peas, seal, meat
3. kite, pine, fly
4. bone, rope, boat
5. mule, cube, suit

Page 77
1. whale
2. tent
3. smile
4. mule
5. stove
6. hay
7. jeep
8. tie
9. frog
10. swing
11. truck
12. van

Page 78
1. drop/dress, drum
2. brush/braid, broom
3. crib/crown, crack
4. track/train, truck
5. frog/frame, fruit

Page 79
1. crab
2. bridge
3. drip
4. bride
5. frog
6. crib
7. pretzel
8. grapes
9. tree
10. frame
11. drill
12. brush

Page 80
1. glue/glove, globe
2. flag/flute, flashlight
3. clock/clip, clap
4. sled/slide, slipper

Answer Key

Page 81

1. clue	2. flag
3. glue	4. flower
5. blanket	6. block
7. slip	8. plant
9. clip	10. glove
11. plate	12. slate

Page 82

1. sw	2. sm
3. st	4. sp
5. sp	6. sw
7. sm	8. sn
9. sn	10. sw
11. st	12. sn
13. st	14. sk
15. sp	16. st

Page 83

1. spell	2. skate
3. smile	4. stick
5. swan	6. stir
7. snake	8. swing
9. snail	10. smell
11. stamp	12. swim

Page 84

1. nt	2. ng	3. ck
4. nd	5. ck	6. ck
7. nt	8. ng	9. ck
10. nd	11. ng	12. ng
13. nt	14. sk	15. nd
16. ck	17. st	18. mp
19. ck	20. sk	

Page 85

1. tree	2. glove
3. flag	4. spoon
5. drum	6. star
7. cloud	8. broom
9. crib	10. plant
11. block	12. swing

Page 86

1. thorn	2. three
3. bath	4. tooth
5. path	

Page 87

1. wheat	2. What
3. whale	4. Where
5. When	

Page 88

1. shovel	2. bush
3. trash	4. shine
5. brush	

Page 89

1. chop	2. cheese
3. bench	4. inch
5. chicken	

Page 90

1. knock	2. knee
3. knight	4. knew
5. knit	

Page 91

1. cheese	2. whale
3. thumb	4. check
5. shark	6. wheel
7. bench	8. fish
9. bath	10. tooth
11. brush	12. watch

Page 92

1. worked	2. fixed
3. washed	4. mowed
5. planted	6. rested

Page 93

1. watering	2. waiting
3. growing	4. picking
5. cooking	6. eating

Page 94

1. fixed	2. helped
3. drawing	4. walking
5. rained	6. barking

Page 95

1. from	2. made
3. your	4. under
5. soon	6. help

Answer Key

Page 96
1. went
2. what
3. find
4. many
5. now
6. again
7. were
8. then
9. much
10. come
11. because
12. over
13. live
14. when

Page 97
1. they
2. get
3. what
4. first
5. was
6. said
7. have
8. want
9. there
10. with
11. again
12. does
13. like
14. went
15. some
16. really
17. come
18. my
19. are
20. walk

Page 98

1.	2	2.	2	3.	3	4.	1
	1		3		2		3
	3		1		1		2
5.	3	6.	2	7.	3	8.	3
	2		1		2		2
	1		3		1		1
9.	1	10.	2	11.	2	12.	3
	3		1		3		1
	2		3		1		2
13.	3	14.	1	15.	2	16.	1
	1		2		3		3
	2		3		1		2

Page 99
1. handbag
2. football
3. raincoat
4. butterfly
5. mailbox
6. pancake

Page 100
1. snowman
2. pinwheel
3. teapot
4. cupcake
5. doghouse
6. starfish

Page 101
1. because
2. come
3. were
4. cupcake
5. again
6. sandbox

Page 102
1. didn't
2. hasn't
3. can't
4. weren't
5. haven't
6. isn't
7. won't
8. aren't
9. don't
10. doesn't

Page 103
1. We're
2. They're
3. You're
4. You're
5. We're
6. They're

Page 104
1. we will
2. they will
3. he will
4. I will
5. it will
6. you will
7. who will

Page 105
1. It's
2. She's
3. He's
4. He's
5. It's

Page 106
1. We're
2. You'll
3. I'm
4. I'll
5. She's
6. can't

Page 107
1. auto
2. little
3. make
4. large
5. shout
6. evening
7. see
8. quick

Page 108
1. under
2. empty
3. thin
4. little
5. weak
6. out
7. wet
8. cold

Answer Key

Page 109
1. pretty
2. tiny
3. long
4. big
5. black
6. small
7. four
8. new

Page 110
1. back
2. unhappy
3. crispy
4. long
5. hop
6. five
7. down
8. day

Page 111
1. 1, 3, 2
2. 3, 1, 2
3. 2, 3, 1

Page 112
2, 1, 4
6, 5, 3

Page 113
1. The birthday party was fun.
2. Sue gave away three kittens.

Page 114
1. Tracy dresses for a rainy day.
2. The old house needs to be fixed.
3. Joey had a good day.

Page 115
Main Idea: It is easy to make a cheese sandwich.
First: Spread butter on two slices of bread.
Next: Put some cheese between the bread slices.
Then: Cut the sandwich in half.
Last: Eat!

Page 116
1. jumped out of bed.
2. stay inside with her family.
3. did the dance well.

Page 117
1. The girl batted the ball through the window.
2. The sun came out.
3. The branch broke off.

Page 118
1. The boy just won a race.
2. The show is done.
3. The girl hears loud noises.
4. Sam just ate a jelly sandwich.
5. This girl does not like carrots.
6. Today is windy.

Page 119
1. Joy's family saw a parade.
2. in town
3. It was good and loud.
4. They will go to the parade.

Page 120
1. Mom and I shop in the city.
2. the school
3. at Main Street
4. Mom and I will go shopping.

Page 121
1., 3., 4., 7., 8., 10.

Page 122
1. The baby is sleeping.
2. We are going to the park.
3. Mom is cooking fish.
4. I am having a party.
5. A bee stung me.
6. Today is a great day.

Page 123
2., 3., 4., 6., 9., 10.

Page 124
1. The sky is blue.
4. It is fun to fly a kite.
6. I like to paint.

Page 125
2., 4., 6., 7., 10.

Page 126
1. May I go with you?
3. What are you doing?
6. What is your favorite movie?

Page 127
3., 5., 6., 7., 9.

Answer Key

Page 128
1. My favorite color is blue.
2. Can we watch a video?
3. Wow that building is tall!
4. I am so hungry!
5. Dad is taking us to the park.
6. Are you feeling ill?

Page 129
1. city
2. farmer
3. flower
4. car
5. shop
6. hat
7. barn
8. girl
9. bug

Page 130
1. Boston
2. Park Road
3. Maria
4. March
5. Japan
6. Ken

Page 131
Animal: lion, horse, frog, tiger, pig
Animals: dogs, rabbits, birds, ducks, cats

Page 132
1. matches
2. buses
3. brushes
4. boxes
5. sixes
6. inches
7. glasses
8. wishes

Page 133
1. sail
2. run
3. sits
4. melts
5. come
6. play
7. throws
8. dives

Page 134
1. wears
2. go
3. get
4. takes
5. floats
6. look

Page 135
1. walks
2. visited
3. watches
4. washing
5. painting
6. purrs

Page 136
The toy car——is broken.
The girls——are best friends.
Snow——is falling on the tree.
My father——is tall.
The dogs——bark loudly.
The store——is open late.

1. Answers will vary.
2. Answers will vary.

Page 137
1. No 2. Yes 3. No 4. No
5. Yes 6. No 7. Yes 8. Yes
9. No 10. Yes

Page 138
1. A frog is in the pond.
2. The movie was funny.
3. Dad and I play catch.
4. Brian can play computer games.
5. He flies a kite on a windy day.
6. I made a card for my mom.

Page 139
1. went
2. ape
3. made
4. bear
5. were
6. ball

Page 140
(Answers may vary.)
1. The dog buried the bone.
2. The king wore a shiny crown.
3. Len sold his card collection.
4. The cat climbed up a tree.
5. A butterfly flew.
6. The baby cried.
7. My little sister sang.

Page 141
1. hand
2. fish
3. soon
4. yes
5. train
6. sled
7. jet
8. six

Answer Key

Page 142
1. mat
2. then
3. club
4. job
5. like
6. boat
7. rain
8. seal

Page 143
1. check
2. flower
3. white
4. band
5. rash
6. moth

Page 144
1. from
2. were
3. working
4. stayed
5. said
6. more
7. does
8. what

Page 145
1. popcorn
2. outside
3. downtown
4. seashell
5. football
6. isn't
7. we're
8. you'll
9. he's
10. don't

Page 146
1. build
2. large
3. shout
4. auto
5. above
6. down
7. huge
8. short
9. night
10. cold

Page 147
1. The city is noisy.
2. She plants flowers.
3. We will have fun visiting Grandma.

Page 148
1. We saw a lot of animals.
2. My Dad likes to fish.
3. Wow! That was a great roller coaster ride!
4. Where would you like to visit?
5. The busy beaver worked and worked.
6. What is your favorite color?
7. Are we riding the bus to school?

Page 149
1. flower
2. boy
3. hop
4. turn
5. tall
6. snowy
7. ducks
8. sing

Page 150
1. On Monday, we are going to the museum.
2. Do you like to eat pie?
3. My Dad is taking a trip to Florida.
4. The little boy chased after the rabbit.
5. An airplane flew through the clouds.
6. Sara wrote a letter to her friend.
7. We watched the sun set.
8. A green lizard ate a bug.
9. The baby smiled at me.